BEATRIX POTTER™ FAVORITE TALES

# THE TALES OF
# PETER RABBIT AND
# JEMIMA PUDDLE-DUCK

*The Original and Authorized Editions by*

## BEATRIX POTTER

FREDERICK WARNE

FREDERICK WARNE

Published by the Penguin Group
Penguin Books Ltd, 80 Strand, London WC2R 0RL, England
Penguin Young Readers Group, 345 Hudson Street, New York, New York 10014, USA
Penguin Group (Canada), 90 Eglinton Avenue East, Suite 700, Toronto, Ontario, Canada M4P 2Y3
Penguin Ireland, 25 St Stephen's Green, Dublin 2, Ireland
Penguin (Group) Australia, 250 Camberwell Road, Camberwell, Victoria 3124, Australia
Penguin Books India (P) Ltd, 11 Community Centre, Panchsheel Park, New Delhi 110 017, India
Penguin Group (NZ), 67 Apollo Drive, Mairangi Bay, Auckland, New Zealand
Penguin Books (South Africa) (Pty) Ltd, P O Box 9, Parklands 2121, South Africa

Penguin Books Ltd, Registered Offices: 80 Strand, London WC2R 0RL, England

Web site at: www.peterrabbit.com

First published by Frederick Warne 2006
5 7 9 10 8 6 4
Copyright © Frederick Warne & Co., 2006
New reproductions of Beatrix Potter's book illustrations copyright © Frederick Warne & Co., 2002
Original text and illustrations copyright © Frederick Warne & Co., 1902, 1908

Frederick Warne & Co. is the owner of all rights, copyrights and trademarks
in the Beatrix Potter character names and illustrations.

ISBN-13: 978 0 7232 5879 7

Printed in China

# CONTENTS

# THE TALE OF
# PETER RABBIT

Once upon a time there were four little Rabbits, and their names were —
Flopsy,
Mopsy,
Cotton-tail,
and Peter.
They lived with their Mother in a sand-bank, underneath the root of a very big fir-tree.

"Now, my dears," said old Mrs. Rabbit one morning, "you may go into the fields or down the lane, but don't go into Mr. McGregor's garden.

"Your Father had
an accident there;
he was put in a pie by
Mrs. McGregor.

"Now run along,
and don't get
into mischief.
I am going out."

Then old Mrs. Rabbit took a basket and her umbrella,
and went through the wood to the baker's. She bought
a loaf of brown bread and five currant buns.

Flopsy, Mopsy and Cotton-tail,
who were good little bunnies, went
down the lane to gather blackberries;

10

But Peter, who was very naughty, ran straight away to Mr. McGregor's garden,

And squeezed under the gate!

First he ate some lettuces and some French beans;
and then he ate some radishes;

And then, feeling rather sick,
he went to look for some parsley.

But round the end of a cucumber frame,
whom should he meet but Mr. McGregor!

Mr. McGregor was on his hands and knees planting out young cabbages, but he jumped up and ran after Peter, waving a rake and calling out, "Stop thief!"

Peter was most dreadfully
frightened; he rushed all
over the garden, for he had
forgotten the way back to the
gate. He lost one of his shoes
among the cabbages,

And the other
shoe amongst
the potatoes.

After losing them, he ran on four legs and went faster, so that I think he might have got away altogether if he had not unfortunately run into a gooseberry net, and got caught by the large buttons on his jacket. It was a blue jacket with brass buttons, quite new.

Peter gave himself up for lost, and shed big tears; but his sobs were overheard by some friendly sparrows, who flew to him in great excitement, and implored him to exert himself.

Mr. McGregor came up with a sieve, which he intended to pop upon the top of Peter; but Peter wriggled out just in time, leaving his jacket behind him,

And rushed into the tool-shed,
and jumped into a can. It would have
been a beautiful thing to hide in, if it
had not had so much water in it.

Mr. McGregor was
quite sure that Peter was
somewhere in the tool-shed,
perhaps hidden underneath
a flower-pot. He began to
turn them over carefully,
looking under each.

Presently Peter sneezed
— "Kertyschoo!"
Mr. McGregor was
after him in no time,

And tried to put his foot upon Peter,
who jumped out of a window,
upsetting three plants. The window
was too small for Mr. McGregor,
and he was tired of running after
Peter. He went back to his work.

Peter sat down to rest; he was out of breath and trembling
with fright, and he had not the least idea which way to go.
Also he was very damp with sitting in that can.

After a time he began to wander about, going lippity —
lippity — not very fast, and looking all round.

He found a door in a wall; but it was locked, and there
was no room for a fat little rabbit to squeeze underneath.

An old mouse was running in and out over the stone door-step, carrying peas and beans to her family in the wood. Peter asked her the way to the gate, but she had such a large pea in her mouth that she could not answer. She only shook her head at him. Peter began to cry.

Then he tried to find his way straight across the garden, but he became more and more puzzled. Presently, he came to a pond where Mr. McGregor filled his water-cans. A white cat was staring at some gold-fish; she sat very, very still, but now and then the tip of her tail twitched as if it were alive. Peter thought it best to go away without speaking to her; he had heard about cats from his cousin, little Benjamin Bunny.

He went back towards the tool-shed, but suddenly, quite close to him, he heard the noise of a hoe — scr-r-ritch, scratch, scratch, scritch. Peter scuttered underneath the bushes.

But presently, as nothing happened, he came out, and climbed upon a wheelbarrow, and peeped over. The first thing he saw was Mr. McGregor hoeing onions. His back was turned towards Peter, and beyond him was the gate!

29

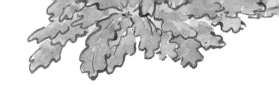

Peter got down very quietly off the wheelbarrow, and
started running as fast as he could go, along a straight
walk behind some blackcurrant bushes.

Mr. McGregor caught sight of him at the corner,
but Peter did not care. He slipped underneath the gate,
and was safe at last in the wood outside the garden.

Mr. McGregor hung up the little jacket and the
shoes for a scarecrow to frighten the blackbirds.

Peter never stopped running
or looked behind him till he
got home to the big fir-tree.

He was so tired that he flopped
down upon the nice soft sand
on the floor of the rabbit-hole,
and shut his eyes. His mother
was busy cooking; she wondered
what he had done with his
clothes. It was the second little
jacket and pair of shoes that
Peter had lost in a fortnight!

I am sorry to say that Peter
was not very well during
the evening.

His mother put him
to bed, and made some
camomile tea; and she
gave a dose of it to Peter!

"One table-spoonful to
be taken at bed-time."

But Flopsy, Mopsy, and Cotton-tail had
bread and milk and blackberries for supper.

## THE END

# THE TALE OF
# JEMIMA
# PUDDLE-DUCK

W̲hat a funny sight it is to see a brood of
ducklings with a hen!
— Listen to the story of Jemima Puddle-duck, who was annoyed
because the farmer's wife would not let her hatch her own eggs.

Her sister-in-law, Mrs. Rebeccah Puddle-duck, was perfectly willing to leave the hatching to some one else — "I have not the patience to sit on a nest for twenty-eight days; and no more have you, Jemima. You would let them go cold; you know you would!"

"I wish to hatch my own eggs; I will hatch them all by myself," quacked Jemima Puddle-duck.

She tried to hide her eggs; but they were always found and carried off.

Jemima Puddle-duck became quite desperate. She determined to make a nest right away from the farm.

She set off on a fine spring afternoon along the cart-road that leads over the hill.

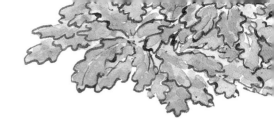

She was wearing
a shawl and a
poke bonnet.

When she reached the
top of the hill, she saw
a wood in the distance.
She thought that it
looked a safe quiet spot.

Jemima Puddle-duck was not much in the habit
of flying. She ran downhill a few yards flapping
her shawl, and then she jumped off into the air.

She flew beautifully when she had got a good start.
She skimmed along over the tree-tops until she saw
an open place in the middle of the wood, where the
trees and brushwood had been cleared.

Jemima alighted rather heavily,
and began to waddle about in search
of a convenient dry nesting-place.
She rather fancied a tree-stump amongst
some tall fox-gloves.

But — seated upon the stump, she was
startled to find an elegantly dressed
gentleman reading a newspaper. He had
black prick ears and sandy-coloured whiskers.
"Quack?" said Jemima Puddle-duck,
with her head and her bonnet on
one side — "Quack?"

The gentleman raised his eyes above his newspaper and looked curiously at Jemima —

"Madam, have you lost your way?" said he. He had a long bushy tail which he was sitting upon, as the stump was somewhat damp.

Jemima thought him mighty civil and handsome. She explained that she had not lost her way, but that she was trying to find a convenient dry nesting-place.

"Ah! is that so? indeed!" said the gentleman with sandy whiskers, looking curiously at Jemima. He folded up the newspaper, and put it in his coat-tail pocket.

Jemima complained of the superfluous hen.

"Indeed? how interesting! I wish I could meet with that fowl. I would teach it to mind its own business!"

"But as to a nest — there is no difficulty: I have a sackful of feathers in my wood-shed. No, my dear madam, you will be in nobody's way. You may sit there as long as you like," said the bushy long-tailed gentleman.

He led the way to a very retired, dismal-looking house amongst the fox-gloves.

It was built of faggots and turf, and there were two broken pails, one on top of another, by way of a chimney.

"This is my summer residence; you would not find my earth — my winter house — so convenient," said the hospitable gentleman.

There was a tumble-down shed at the back of the house, made of old soap-boxes. The gentleman opened the door, and showed Jemima in.

The shed was almost quite full of feathers — it was almost suffocating; but it was comfortable and very soft. Jemima Puddle-duck was rather surprised to find such a vast quantity of feathers. But it was very comfortable; and she made a nest without any trouble at all.

When she came out, the sandy-whiskered gentleman was sitting on a log reading the newspaper — at least he had it spread out, but he was looking over the top of it. He was so polite, that he seemed almost sorry to let Jemima go home for the night. He promised to take great care of her nest until she came back again next day.

He said he loved eggs and ducklings; he should be proud to see a fine nestful in his wood-shed.

Jemima Puddle-duck came every afternoon; she laid nine eggs in the nest. They were greeny white and very large. The foxy gentleman admired them immensely. He used to turn them over and count them when Jemima was not there.

At last Jemima told him that she intended to begin to sit next day
— "and I will bring a bag of corn with me, so that I need never
leave my nest until the eggs are hatched. They might catch cold,"
said the conscientious Jemima.

"Madam, I beg you not to trouble yourself with a bag; I will provide oats. But before you commence your tedious sitting, I intend to give you a treat. Let us have a dinner-party all to ourselves! May I ask you to bring up some herbs from the farm-garden to make a savoury omelette? Sage and thyme, and mint and two onions, and some parsley. I will provide lard for the stuff — lard for the omelette," said the hospitable gentleman with sandy whiskers.

Jemima Puddle-duck was a simpleton: not even the mention of sage and onions made her suspicious. She went round the farm-garden, nibbling off snippets of all the different sorts of herbs that are used for stuffing roast duck.

And she waddled into the kitchen, and got two onions out of a basket.

The collie-dog Kep met her coming out. "What are you doing with those onions? Where do you go every afternoon by yourself, Jemima Puddle-duck?"

Jemima was rather in awe of the collie; she told him the whole story.

The collie listened, with his wise head on one side; he grinned when she described the polite gentleman with sandy whiskers.

He asked several questions about the wood, and about the exact position of the house and shed.

Then he went out, and trotted down the village.
He went to look for two fox-hound puppies
who were out at walk with the butcher.

56

Jemima Puddle-duck went up the cart-road for the last time, on a sunny afternoon. She was rather burdened with bunches of herbs and two onions in a bag.

She flew over the wood, and alighted opposite the house of the bushy long-tailed gentleman.

He was sitting on a log; he sniffed the air, and kept glancing uneasily round the wood. When Jemima alighted he quite jumped.

"Come into the house as soon
as you have looked at your eggs.
Give me the herbs for the omelette.
Be sharp!"

He was rather abrupt. Jemima
Puddle-duck had never heard
him speak like that.

She felt surprised,
and uncomfortable.

While she was inside she heard pattering feet round the back of the shed. Some one with a black nose sniffed at the bottom of the door, and then locked it.

Jemima became much alarmed.

A moment afterwards there were most awful noises — barking, baying, growls and howls, squealing and groans.

And nothing more was ever seen of that
foxy-whiskered gentleman.

Presently Kep opened the door of the shed,
and let out Jemima Puddle-duck.

Unfortunately the puppies rushed in and
gobbled up all the eggs before he could stop them.

He had a bite on his ear and both the puppies
were limping.

Jemima Puddle-duck was escorted home in
tears on account of those eggs.

She laid some more in June, and she was permitted
to keep them herself; but only four of them hatched.
    Jemima Puddle-duck said that it was because of
her nerves; but she had always been a bad sitter.

### THE END